The Yellow House

by

Liliah Raye

Copyright © 2019

All Rights Reserved. No part of this publication may be reproduced, stored in a retrieval system or transmitted, in any form or by any means, electronic, mechanical, photocopying, recording or otherwise, without the written permission of the copyright holder.

To Sputnik, my spooky cat

Chapter 1

It was the middle of July in the year 2002. After placing her suitcase in the trunk of her car at 6 am, Miranda started the engine. She was leaving the city and heading to the countryside to spend some days alone at her parents' summer cottage.

Miranda was a pretty and slim 23-year-old woman. She was five feet and three inches tall and had blue eyes and dyed-blue hair past her shoulders. She worked as a hairdresser in a salon close to her apartment. It was the beginning of the young hairdresser's three-week vacation for the summer, and she felt it couldn't have come soon enough.

The cottage was approximately twenty-five miles away. Forty minutes later, the city was far behind her and she was driving through the scenic rural area of the country. The roads were still smooth and the morning sun lit the lush, green vegetation on both sides. The homes were a good distance apart from one another and several of them were farmhouses. She winded down the glass so she could breathe the cool, fresh morning air.

A few minutes after 7 am, Miranda reached her destination. She parked in the garage of the cottage and took her bags inside. The cottage was clean and its distinct Cherry wood smell brought back many fond memories of past vacations with her parents. The left part of the cottage contained a living room and a kitchen, and the right part had two small bedrooms and a bathroom.

After calling her parents' home to let them know she had arrived at the cottage safely, Miranda opened two windows – one in the living room and one in the front bedroom. The windows had screens on them to prevent mosquitoes from getting inside. Afterwards, she plugged on the refrigerator in the kitchen, packed some food and drinks in it, and then made the bed.

When she had finished making the bed, she walked outside. There was a large and clean lake right in front of the cottage. On the bank to the right was an old wooden boat. She recalled the many fishing trips she had gone on with her father, while growing up. On the other side of the lake, there was a thick forest. All around her, many shrubs, flowers and trees grew wild. As the breeze blew gently though the trees above and through her long hair, she walked to the edge of the lake and seated herself on a large rock. It was her favourite sitting spot. There, she began to slowly take in the beauty of the atmosphere and allow the rays of the sun to bathe her.

Several minutes later, Miranda turned her gaze to the far right of the cottage. Through the trees, she could make out a two-storey yellow house. Although there was nothing unusual about the appearance of the house, it was a building that haunted her since she could remember. There was an eerie and mysterious energy about the house that raised the hairs on her arms. It also seemed fearfully quiet, like someone who knew secrets that were too dangerous to divulge. Because she had seen lights in the house at nights in the past, she knew people lived there, but she knew nothing about them. Miranda had always been curious about the yellow house, and the more she looked at it, the hungrier she felt for answers.

Brushing her thoughts off, Miranda lay back on the smooth and flat rock and closed her eyes. She reminded herself of her intention to keep her mind completely peaceful throughout her stay at the cottage.

In the afternoon, Miranda ate lunch and then took a nap. When she woke up, she saw it was some minutes after 4 pm, and thought it was a good time to go swimming. She put on a blue two-piece bathing suit and walked into the lake, feeling the stones pressing against the bottoms of her feet, and the cool, refreshing water on her skin. She continued walking into the water until the water level reached her breasts, and then she completely immersed herself under the water. She swam there beneath the surface for a quarter of a minute and observed a few gray trout that swam by. To Miranda, being under water always felt magical. It was a feeling of becoming one with the water itself.

After swimming, she changed and sat on a chair in the porch with some green tea. Suddenly, a beautiful black cat walked onto the porch and sat just a few feet away from her. Miranda found that it had the cutest paws, and noticed the front left one was white. It didn't meow, but stared at her in a relaxed way with its bright copper eyes.

"Oh, hello," Miranda said sweetly. "You must be hungry."

Miranda loved animals and couldn't resist feeding a stray cat or dog. She went in and returned with a piece of cooked fish in a little plastic plate. The cat looked up at Miranda as she placed the plate in front of it. After sniffing the fish a few times, the cat nibbled on it, then licked its lips and walked off the porch. Moments later, the strange animal was out of sight.

Chapter 2

At 5 am the next morning, Miranda woke up suddenly after a terrifying dream. Her heart was beating fast and she felt an urgency to recall the dream. When she began to calm her mind, she remembered what she had dreamt. In the dream she was walking through a dark and slightly winding tunnel. It was cold and very dimly lit by natural light that was coming from behind her. After walking for what felt like a couple of minutes, she saw an old man sitting against the wall, with his head down. He was frail and had grey hair up to his shoulders. The man seemed non-threatening, and looked up as Miranda approached him. When their eyes met, she saw a great deal of worry and sadness in his face.

"Please help me," he pleaded, hoarsely. "Help me out of here…"

"Come with me," Miranda stretched out her hand to the old man. "If we walk towards the source of the light, we'll be out of here."

"No," he shook his head with fear in his eyes. "Whenever I try to go towards the light, they come and drag me back here…"

"Who?"

"The shadow beings," he whispered in a tone of despair.

Miranda saw that he was too scared to move from where he was.

"How can I help you then?"

"Her spell needs to be broken."

"Who's spell?"

Before the frail old man could answer, Miranda noticed three pale beings coming towards her from the darker part of the tunnel. Their menacing eyes glowed white from under their black hoods, and they seemed to float about a foot off the ground.

"Let's get out of here," Miranda panicked.

She quickly gestured to the man but he shook his head again and didn't budge.

"Run, girl!" He cried out.

As the entities chased her, Miranda ran as fast as she could through the tunnel, towards the light. As soon as she reached the tunnel's exit, she woke up.

The dream remained at the back of her mind throughout the day. It had felt very real. In the evening, she sat down on a chair in the porch after her swim in the lake and wondered who the man could be. She figured that maybe if she said a prayer for his freedom, it would help. A minute after she finished her prayer, the black cat appeared again on her porch. It sat right where she was, and stared at her with its piercing copper eyes. When Miranda reached out to pet the beautiful creature, it affectionately rubbed its face against her hand.

Before Miranda got up to get something for it to eat, the little copper-eyed animal jumped off the porch and peered back at her. It walked forward a little and looked at her again. Having a strong feeling that the mysterious cat wanted her to follow it, she slipped on her flip flops and stepped down from the porch. When the cat turned to the right and headed into the thicker part of the woods, Miranda hesitated, took a deep breath and began to walk behind it. The cat led her along a very narrow, meandering path through the woods. The air felt cooler and several birds were flying above them, from tree to tree. The area was filled with huge trees, shrubs, dried logs and moss-covered rocks. Soon they came to a small stream. There was a line of rocks that stretched from one end of the stream's bank to the other, forming a short dry bridge. Miranda watched as the cat walked along the top of the rocks to get to the other side, and she stealthily did the same. After they crossed the stream, the land inclined, steadily. As she ascended the small hill, Miranda wished she had worn better footwear.

In seconds, a house came into view. It was no ordinary one. It was the yellow house that had always haunted Miranda. It was just fifty feet away from her. She had never been so close to the house before. She paused, feeling her heart starting to race. The cat, sensing her fear, turned around and meowed. It was a soft and encouraging meow. The cat slowly made its way to the top of the hill, and Miranda continued behind, feeling her legs shaking slightly.

When Miranda reached to the top of the hill, she was facing the side of the house which was just about twenty-five feet away. As she observed the place, she found herself frozen in reluctant fascination. While she stood there, the cat ran to the house, jumped through a window and disappeared. Suddenly, she noticed a branch from a tree in the yard was shaking. Seconds later, a cute young woman slowly climbed down from the tree with a fruit in her hand. She was thin, five feet and six inches tall, had long, straight and light brown hair and was wearing a pair of blue jeans and a white T shirt. Miranda watched her bite into the fruit. At first, Miranda thought to leave but then realized she had already been spotted.

Miranda slowly and nervously waved to the brunette. When she saw this, she made her way to Miranda.

"Are you lost?" The brunette asked when she came up to Miranda. She had never in her life seen a stranger in that area of the woods.

"No, I... I was just hiking," the blue-haired woman replied.

Miranda noticed that the fruit the young woman was eating was a nectarine. The juice glistened on her lips and ran down her arm.

"I'm Jess," the brunette put her hand out to greet Miranda. "I live here."

Miranda found that Jess' voice was deep, soft and attractive. She also couldn't help but notice the brunette's beautiful mouth and intense hazel eyes.

"I'm Miranda."

"Nice hair," Jess said after they shook hands.

"Thanks," the blue-haired woman said. "I'm staying for some days in my parents' cottage down that way."

Jess looked in the direction in which she was pointing.

"Ah, you're staying in that place in front of the lake."

"You know it?"

"Yeah, I row past there occasionally when I go fishing," Jess said. "I think I saw you there with your parents one or two summers ago... I saw the bushes there recently. They could use some pruning."

"Yes, I really need to get them trimmed."

"I do yard work if you're interested."

"Oh, how much do you charge?"

"I'd prune the bushes and clean up the weeds around the place for fifty dollars," Jess replied. "The job will take two days."

"Sounds great," Miranda responded. "When can you start?"

"I can start tomorrow morning at 9 am if you'd like."

"See you tomorrow then, Jess," Miranda turned and began to head down the hill.

"There's a road that will take you back to your cottage, faster," Jess informed her. "Just walk to your right and you'll find it in less than a minute."

"Thank you," Miranda was relieved that she didn't have to trek back through the thick woods.

As she turned and walked towards the road, she glanced to her left and saw the side of the yellow house. She immediately experienced chills and had a feeling like she was being watched. Soon she arrived on the road. She turned right and headed back to the cottage.

Chapter 3

The next day, Jess arrived at the cottage a few minutes before 9 am. After turning off the engine of her old, white pickup truck, she took out her equipment and walked to the front of the cottage. She was wearing a red shirt and blue jeans, and brought with her a large clipper, a pair of garden-gloves, a chainsaw and a few other items. When she called out to Miranda, the blue-haired woman answered and came out to meet her. She wore a light blue knee-high dress with thin shoulder straps.

"Would you like some breakfast or something to drink?" Miranda asked Jess.

"Thanks, but maybe later," Jess said. "I should get to work."

"Alright then," Miranda replied.

After Miranda told her what she wanted to be pruned, trimmed and weeded, Jess put on her gloves and began to start up her chainsaw.

"Just call me if you need anything," Miranda said.

The brunette nodded and started working.

An hour later, Miranda came out on the porch with a cup of coffee and admired Jess' skillfulness. She was delighted by the clean and neat appearance of the newly trimmed plants and the beautiful way the light was coming through them.

When it was 11 am, Jess walked over to Miranda and told her she'd come by the next day at the same time to finish the task.

"I made some fish sandwiches and lemonade," the blue-haired woman said. "Would you come have lunch with me?"

"Sure," Jess nodded and went inside with Miranda.

After using the washroom to wash her hands, Jess joined Miranda at the table. They sat opposite to each other and began eating.

"This is good," the brunette said after taking a bite of her sandwich.

"Glad you like it," Miranda poured them some lemonade. "So, do you live there by yourself, Jess?"

"I live there with my mother and grandfather," replied the brunette before taking another bite. "I've lived there all of my life. Are you and your parents from the city?"

"Yes, my parents and I are from the city, but I live a few miles away from them, in my own apartment," replied the blue-haired woman. "If you don't mind me asking, how old are you?"

"I'm 19," Jess replied. "What about you? You don't look much older than I am."

"I'm 23," Miranda chuckled. "In the city, I do hairdressing in a salon. Do you go to school, Jess?"

"Well," Jess took a drink of lemonade, "when I have enough money saved up, I plan to move out and attend culinary school."

"Oh, that's lovely."

Jess paused for a few moments, "Well, it won't be lovely for my mom."

"Why do you say that?" The blue-haired woman asked.

"She doesn't want me to move out."

"She's concerned about your safety?"

"No, it's not that," Jess shook her head. "I do most of the work in and outside of the house. She wants me to stay and continue to clean, cook, wash and garden. She's in her forties and quite able to take care of herself."

"I see," Miranda frowned. "Well, you need to follow your heart and live your life. After you move out, she'll get used to the idea that you're living your life, and she'll be alright."

"It won't be that easy..." Jess replied somberly.

"Why not?" Miranda was concerned.

"Have you heard about my mother?" Jess asked. "You must have heard some things."

"I haven't…" the blue-haired woman replied. "Besides you, I don't know about anyone else from around here. What about her?"

"I don't know if you'd believe me, but she's a witch," the brunette said.

"A witch?" Miranda's blue eyes widened.

"Yes, and *not* the good kind," responded Jess. "She does it for a living. People… well, bad people, come from all over to seek her help."

"You're afraid of her."

"I've seen what she can do," Jess said. "When I was little, she felt that someone cheated her at the market and she caused all of his livestock to die in a week. A few years ago, a woman not far from here told her that she'd burn in hell. That same afternoon, my mother put a curse on her. Within a month, the woman succumbed to a strange illness and died shortly afterwards. I think she killed her sister too. I never saw her do any spell against her, but I know she hated her. Also, a healthy 30-something-year-old woman doesn't just die in her sleep. I've also seen this thing she does. If she wants to find out something, she calls the names of certain spirits and sends them to get information for her."

Although, she had never heard stories like that, Miranda saw the sincerity in Jess' eyes and she believed every word Jess was telling her.

"She said if I leave her," Jess continued, "she would destroy me."

"There must be something you can do to protect yourself... or prevent her from harming people ever again."

"I'll have to find a way," said the brunette. "I've been doing a lot of research lately, at the library... I'll find a way."

Jess sounded hopeful. Miranda was impressed by Jess' positivity and determination.

"So, you're saving the money you make doing yard-work for your tuition?"

"Besides the yard-work, I paint houses and sell eggs from my chickens," Jess said. "I can do home renovations too."

"Wow," Miranda raised her eyebrows. "How did you learn to do renovations?"

"My grandfather taught me..." Jess replied. "Two and a half months ago, he was diagnosed with fourth-stage lung cancer."

"I'm sorry to hear that," Miranda said. "Is your grandfather alive?" She asked softly.

"Yes," said Jess. "He's alive and he's also cancer free."

"That's wonderful news," Miranda said joyfully. "Fourth-stage cancer is very hard to beat."

"My mother did a ritual to cure him," Jess said. "He's her dad. It's not really love but more like… an *attachment* she has for him. I don't think she's capable of loving anyone."

"Well, I'm glad that he's cured," the blue-haired woman responded.

"He's cured, yes, and healthy too, but he's not the same," said the brunette. "My mother insists that he's Okay, but it seems to me that he's not himself."

Miranda heard sadness in Jess' tone and sensed the brunette shared a close bond with her grandfather. There was a pause for a few moments as Miranda wondered what could have caused Jess to think her grandfather wasn't himself. The blue-haired woman knew that severe illness could change most people.

"I hope he's back to his normal self soon," Miranda said. "If there's anything I can do to help, let me know."

"Thanks for offering to help, Miranda," the cute brunette said. "Thank you also for listening. You're the first person I've opened up to about my family…"

"You're welcome," the blue-haired woman said empathically. "I'm here for you."

When they had finished their meal, Miranda walked the brunette to the porch and paid her twenty-five dollars which was half the total for the job. In the bright afternoon light, Miranda caught Jess looking at the pink mosquito bites on her arm.

"The bugs here are brutal," Miranda rubbed her arms.

"Did you bring repellant?"

"I completely forgot it..."

"I'll bring some for you tomorrow," the brunette said.

"Oh, that would be very much appreciated," said Miranda.

While they stood on the porch, Miranda remembered the cat and wondered if it would come by later.

"You have a gorgeous cat by the way," the blue-haired woman told Jess.

"Cat?" The brunette looked a bit bewildered. "I don't have a cat..."

"I saw it run into your house," Miranda said. "It's a black cat with bright copper eyes and a white paw. It visits me."

"Cats don't come around my home, unfortunately," the brunette said.

Miranda knew she couldn't have imagined the cat.

After Jess collected the equipment she brought with her, she promised to visit the next day at 9 am to finish the job.

Chapter 4

Miranda awoke a few minutes past 6 the next morning, had a quick shower, put on a shorts and a loose-fitting tee shirt, and then made her way to her favourite rock by the lake. After climbing on top of it, she sat cross-legged and had a twenty-minute meditation session. Nothing was more peaceful and relaxing to her than meditating in nature while breathing the cool and clean air and soaking in the gentle rays of the sun. When her session was over, she felt very calm, light and energized. A short while later, Miranda prepared pancakes and tea. She took her breakfast out on the porch with a romance novel.

Jess arrived promptly at 9. When the blue-haired woman heard the door of Jess' vehicle shut, she put down her novel and went out to meet her. Jess' hair was out, as usual, and she wore a blue jeans with a light-blue shirt tucked in it and sneakers. She was pulling out her equipment from the tray of the old, white pickup. As Miranda approached Jess, the brunette turned and they greeted each other with a smile. It was the first time Miranda saw Jess smile. The brunette's sexy, boyish smile made her heart skip a beat and gave her an intense feeling in her tummy.

"Nice vehicle," Miranda said.

Jess looked at her to see if she was talking about her old pickup.

"This was one of my grandfather's vehicles," Jess said. "He gave it to me after I got my driver's license. It has some age but it takes me where I need to go."

"May I help you with your stuff?"

Jess paused for a moment and then handed Miranda her backpack.

When they got to the yard, they rested the bag and tools down. Jess then opened her bag and pulled out a small, clear vial that contained some light-green liquid.

"Repellant for you," she handed the vial to Miranda.

"Oh, thank you so much," Miranda took the vial and examined the light-green liquid. "Interesting… Did you buy this?"

"I made it myself using essential oils and herbs I grow in my yard," Jess said. "It's good for getting rid of negative energy too… if you believe in that stuff."

The blue-haired woman opened the little cork and dabbed a bit on her fingers. The fragrance was strong, but pleasing.

"Where did you learn about oils and herbs?" Miranda rubbed a little of the liquid on her arms. "Did your mother teach you?"

"No," the brunette replied. "I learned about them from books I read at the library," Jess said.

"That's lovely," Miranda replied. "Would you like some of the repellant? The mosquitoes out here are relentless."

"No, thank you," the brunette replied. "Mosquitoes don't seem to like me much."

Miranda chuckled, "Okay, well I don't want to keep you from your work. I'll be inside if you need me."

Two hours later, Jess finished the job and called out to Miranda from the porch. When the blue-haired woman came out, Jess took her around the cottage and showed her the work she did. The place looked clean, neat and beautiful. She noticed that the hedges were trimmed and each tree was pruned. She also saw that all of the weeds on the ground and the unsightly vines that were crawling on the outside walls were gone. It made her recall the way it used to look when she was a child and she was filled with nostalgia. She was beyond happy with the job Jess did for her.

"The place looks amazing," Miranda told Jess when they returned to the front of the cottage.

The blue-haired woman handed Jess the rest of the cash and thanked her for her work.

"I'm glad you're happy," Jess smiled and began to gather up her tools and equipment.

"Would you have lunch with me?" Miranda asked. "I made some macaroni and cheese. It's not the box kind. I prepared it from scratch."

"Okay," Jess nodded and followed Miranda.

When they arrived on the porch, the novel the blue-haired woman was reading caught Jess' eyes. It lay on the little table in the porch with its front cover exposed. On the cover, two pretty young women were tangled in an intimate embrace in the woods. When Miranda turned and saw Jess looking at it, she blushed and quickly picked it up.

After using the washroom to freshen up, Jess found Miranda at the table and helped herself to some macaroni and cheese. Miranda had already poured them some apple juice.

"This is really good," the brunette remarked. "Very creamy and delicious…"

"Thanks, I'm happy you like it."

"By the way, your bathroom door needs fixing," Jess said.

"Yeah," Miranda swallowed. "It's rubbing on the floor. I'd have to take care of that."

"I can fix it for you, if you want."

"Oh, how much would it cost?"

"I'd do it for you for free," the brunette replied. "I can come by tomorrow, after lunch."

"Thank you so much, Jess," Miranda said.

They ate happily while sharing a bit of small talk. Jess finished her plate first and waited patiently until Miranda finished hers. The brunette then reached into her wallet and pulled out a photograph of her on a sofa, holding a black cat.

"The cat you saw," Jess placed the photo on the table, "did it look like this one?"

"Oh my goodness," the blue-haired woman responded on seeing the picture. "Those eyes... Same white paw... Yes, this is the cat I saw."

"That's Oliver," Jess said pointing to the cat she was holding in the photograph.

"But you told me you didn't own any cats..."

"I don't," the brunette responded. "Oliver died two years ago. He was old."

Miranda's jaw dropped, "But I saw..."

"I believe you," Jess said softly. "You have a gift."

The blue-haired woman sat back in her chair, speechless. Her eyes were fixed on the picture. The brunette pulled out another photo from her wallet, and gently placed it next to the first. It showed Oliver lying next to an old man on a bed. The old man was reading a newspaper and the cat was licking its paw.

"That's my grandfather," Jess pointed to the man in the photo. "Oliver loved him. He rescued Ollie from a ditch when he was just about three weeks old."

In an instant, Miranda recognized the man in the picture. It was the old man from her dream! Miranda's breath was caught in her throat and she turned pale.

"What's wrong?" Jess asked.

"I dreamed him."

"You dreamed my grandfather?"

"Yes, three nights ago."

"What did you dream?"

"I was walking through a dark tunnel and saw him sitting there, by himself," Miranda began. "He looked sad and worried and asked me to help him. When I tried to help him out of the place, some demonic spirits with hoods started to chase after me."

"The spirits, did they have white, glowing eyes?"

"Yes."

"Were they wearing black hoods? Jess asked. "And did they float?"

"Yes," The blue-haired woman said. "You've dreamt them too?"

"Yes," Jess replied. "A few times I dreamed them around my mother. I think those are the spirits she works with."

"I just remembered something," Miranda said. "In the dream, your grandfather said someone's spell needs to be broken for him to be free."

Jess nodded, "It makes sense now…"

"What do you mean?"

"The ritual my mother did to heal him caused him to be possessed by the evil entities with the glowing eyes," Jess said. "They healed him, but they also went into his body… and that's why he's not the same."

"And to save him, the spell she did needs to be broken," Miranda added.

"Maybe I can find a book in the library that will help me with this," Jess placed the photos back into her wallet and stood up.

"Are you going to the library now?"

"Yes," Jess replied. "Would you like to come with me?"

"Sure," Miranda said, "let me get my bag."

Chapter 5

As soon as they packed Jess' equipment into her vehicle, the brunette opened the passenger door for Miranda. The blue-haired woman found it was a sweet gesture. She thanked Jess and tried not to blush. When they were both seated, Jess started the engine and told Miranda that the library was about four miles away.

Along the way, they passed many country homes, farm houses, an old Pentecostal church and a small elementary school.

"My grandfather and I painted that school last year," the brunette pointed to the peach-coloured school.

After a few minutes of driving through the countryside, they arrived in front of a wooden building with large and beautiful mahogany doors. It seemed like it had been there for a century and its structure was quite strong.

When they entered the library, a tall and slim middle-aged man at the librarian's desk looked up from his book and smiled. He wore thin-framed glasses and had light coloured hair and a peaceful demeanour.

"Good afternoon, Jessica," the librarian's voice matched his appearance.

"Good afternoon Walter," the brunette replied. "I brought a friend with me today. Her name is Miranda."

"How can I help you ladies today?" Walter asked.

"Well," said Jess, "we're looking for books on how to save someone from demonic possession. Do you have any books like that?"

Walter thought for some seconds and then rose from his chair.

"Follow me," he replied.

Jess and Miranda followed Walter up a wooden staircase to the second floor. He then led them into a room filled with occult books of all kinds. They walked through the room until they came to a locked door that was located at the back of the room.

The tall man pulled out a bunch of keys from his pocket, "I believe you'll find what you're looking for in here."

When Walter opened the door, there was a mild scent of old books. The small room hadn't been opened in many years. He reached in and flicked the light switch. In the room, there were three shelves of aged hard-cover and paperback books and one rectangular table with a few chairs.

"The books in this room cannot be borrowed," the librarian informed them. "I trust you will use the information you find within them wisely…"

"We will," Jess said. "Thank you."

"Good luck ladies," Walter said before heading back to his desk.

Miranda and Jess got to work immediately. They spent fifteen minutes searching through the shelves and selecting books they thought had information on banishing demons. After placing eighteen books on the table, they sat down, facing each other, and began to go through them. Miranda pulled out a notepad and a pen from her handbag so they could write down information.

The young women were amazed at the things revealed in the books as well as the drawings within them. In those books, there was so much information on the spiritual realm and its various types of inhabitants. There were also interesting symbols, potions, spells and rituals. About an hour later, Miranda looked up from an open hard-cover book.

"I've found something," the blue-haired woman said.

"What is it?" Jess asked.

"It looks like a potion to expel evil spirits from a person..."

The brunette got up and went over to Miranda. She sat down next to her and carefully studied the page.

"This should work," Jess whispered.

"Do you have all of the ingredients?"

"Not all of them, but I can source the ones I don't have from places nearby," Jess said as she began to write down the ingredients for the potion. "After I prepare the potion, I have to chant this spell here three times to bless it, and then have my granddad consume nine drops of it. I'll make it today and give him it."

"Won't he be suspicious of what you're giving him?"

"I'll put it in his tea or dinner," Jess said. "It's not so strong so he won't suspect anything."

A few minutes later, after Jess had written down the necessary information, they put the books back in their places on the shelves and left the room. After thanking Walter, they left the library, got into the vehicle and began to head back.

On their way back, Jess took a right turn and stopped off at the farmer's market to buy a few herbs for the potion. Miranda accompanied her and helped her to find the items. Afterwards, they went to a store on the same street. There, Jess purchased a couple more things.

"Do you have everything you need?" Miranda asked Jess when they returned to the vehicle.

"Yes," the brunette restarted the engine.

"I hope it works," Miranda said as she placed her hand gently on Jess' shoulder.

"Me too…" Jess responded, hopefully.

After Jess dropped her back to the cottage, Miranda went for a swim and then spent some time in the porch. The atmosphere was a lot cleaner and more relaxing than it was before. As she looked around, she wondered if she would see Oliver again.

That night before Miranda drifted off to sleep in her bed, all she could think of was Jess. She hoped that Jess was successful in freeing her grandfather from the dark entities. Soon, Miranda drifted off to sleep, and she suddenly found herself in the same dark tunnel again. After walking down the tunnel for less than a minute, she found Jess' grandfather. He was sitting on the floor in the same place, with a depressed and gloomy expression. Suddenly, the blue-haired woman spotted some movement not too far ahead, in the darker part of the tunnel. In seconds, the three pale, floating entities appeared again. Their glowing eyes seemed much more angry and threatening than before. Miranda immediately started to panic. Instinctively, she grabbed the old man's wrist.

"We can get out of here if we move fast enough," Miranda's tone was urgent.

"No, they won't let us," his eyes showed fear. "The spell, it needs to be broken."

The beings were rapidly drawing nearer and Miranda saw that he wasn't going to budge.

"You need to get out of this place!" Jess' grandfather shouted. "Run!"

As Miranda turned and ran towards the exit, the beings ran after her. This time, they were a great deal closer to her than the time before. Seconds later, one of the demons grabbed her by the waist. Miranda kicked and screamed as it started to drag her back into the darker part of the tunnel. She could feel its long nails digging into her back and tummy. All of a sudden, a bright yellow light came bursting through the tunnel's exit. It was a warm and supernatural light that illuminated the entire tunnel and everything in it. In an instant, the diabolical being let go of Miranda, and all three of the demons started letting out loud, high-pitched sounds of agony. They couldn't bear the light, not for a moment. With widened eyes, the blue-haired woman watched as the light quickly incinerated them, and saw their dust settle on the floor of the tunnel.

All was silent for a few moments, and then Miranda heard the footsteps of someone coming towards her. In a short time, Jess' grandfather came into view, and he was beaming with joy. Miranda smiled too and they began walking out of the tunnel together. As soon as they both exited the tunnel, the blue-haired woman woke up.

Chapter 6

At about half past one the next afternoon, Jess showed up at the cottage wearing a white T-shirt and black shorts. She brought tools and other items to fix Miranda's bathroom door. When the blue haired woman heard Jess call from the porch, the blue-haired woman came out to invite her in.

"So," Miranda said when they reached inside, "did you make the potion yesterday?"

"I did," Jess put her backpack on the couch in the living room.

"Tell me what happened," Miranda gestured for Jess to sit on the couch.

After they were seated next to each other, Jess began to describe the incident.

"It took me about an hour to prepare everything," Jess started, "and afterwards I added it to my granddad's tea. He usually has a cup of tea before her goes to bed. I told him I'd make it for him, and I did. I added exactly nine drops to his tea and took it to his room... I sat on the chair in the room and stayed with him for a while. Less than a minute after he finished his tea, he started coughing. It wasn't normal coughing. It was a loud and non-stop dry cough that sounded like he was trying to dislodge something from his lungs. It went on for over a minute and I thought he was going to pass out."

"Did you try to help him?"

"I offered to get him some water and he nodded," Jess replied. "I fetched the water as quickly as I could. When I returned to his room, he was lying still on his bed with his eyes closed. I tried shaking him and calling him but he didn't answer me. My heart was pounding in my chest... Seconds later, he opened his eyes."

"Oh thank goodness," Miranda exhaled.

"When he eventually spoke, his voice was weak," Jess said. "He said right after my mother did the ritual for him to be healed, he fell into a dark place and was held as a prisoner by wicked spirits. I told him I realized he wasn't himself. He said the demons were destroyed a short while after he drank the tea. I told him I put a potion I made into the tea and he said he realized I did that. He then asked if I knew a girl with blue hair. I told him about you and what you did to help me. He's very thankful for what we did and he said he'd like to meet you soon."

"That would be wonderful," Miranda responded. "I'm just so happy he's alright now."

"Me too," Jess smiled. "He said he won't let his daughter perform any spell or ritual for him ever again. I used to tell my granddad that she used evil spirits to do her bidding but he didn't believe me. He does now."

"Do you think your mother made him demon-possessed on purpose?"

"I don't think she did, or that she knew he was demon-possessed," the brunette replied. "But I do know she won't hesitate to do that to someone she doesn't like…"

"I see," the blue-haired woman said.

"Anyway, Miranda, I should get started on the door."

Jess rose to her feet and opened her knapsack. There was a much more relaxed energy about Jess and Miranda felt it. Miranda asked Jess if she'd have some lemonade with her before she started to work and the brunette nodded and thanked her. While they had some lemonade, the brunette explained why the bathroom door was rubbing on the floor. She said that the old hinges were the problem because they were causing the door to sag.

When Jess began fixing the door, the blue-haired woman offered to help but Jess told her she could handle it on her own. Miranda brought a chair close to where Jess was, sat down and observed the process. As Miranda watched Jess work expertly and with confidence on the door, with her strong hands and their long fingers, she felt her insides get hot. Miranda wasn't one to be turned on easily. She found herself fighting the thoughts of Jess' hands on her body.

"Can I ask you a personal question, Jess?"

"Sure," the brunette worked on removing the second hinge.

"Do you have a boyfriend?"

"Nope," Jess turned her head to Miranda. "Boys aren't my type... I thought you'd have picked up on that by now."

Miranda smiled, "So, do you have a girlfriend?"

"I don't have anyone," Jess said. "What about you?"

"Same here," Miranda responded.

It took Jess less than fifteen minutes to replace the old hinges with new ones that she had brought with her. When she was finished, the door opened and closed perfectly, and Miranda happily thanked her.

"It's very hot today," Miranda remarked. "A good day to go swimming... Would you join me?"

"Sounds great," replied Jess, "but I didn't bring a bath suit or towel."

"I have one you can borrow," Miranda replied, "and there are towels in the closet. Come with me."

Jess followed her friend into the bedroom. On the bed, Miranda laid three two-pieces for Jess to choose from. At first the brunette was hesitant because she had never worn a two-piece, but she eventually selected one. It was light-purple. Miranda chose one that was orange in colour.

They changed facing away from each other, and then headed out the door.

When they stepped into the lake, the blue-haired woman was amazed at Jess' beautifully toned body.

"Do you play sports, Jess?"

"Well, I used to play soccer in school, a couple years ago."

"Oh," Miranda looked curious. "Do you work out?"

"Occasionally…"

The combination of the afternoon sun, the fresh, cool water and the gentle summer breezes was very enjoyable for both of them. They swam in the shallow part of the lake for a while, and afterwards, they decided to swim to the deeper part of the lake. When Miranda reached the area that was about ten feet deep, she turned around and treaded the water. Looking around, she saw no sign of Jess. Miranda glanced around frantically for three seconds and was about to dive under the water to look for her friend when suddenly someone grabbed her by the ankle. In an instant, Jess popped up from the water in front of her, laughing.

"Jess, you scared me!"

"Got you, didn't I," Jess laughed, finding Miranda's angry tone to be cute.

A few moments later, the blue-haired woman calmed down.

"Who taught you how to swim?" Miranda asked.

"No one," the brunette said. "Did someone teach you?"

"My mom taught me," Miranda said, "right here in this lake."

"Oh, that's great."

After treading the water for a few minutes, they swam back to the bank and then sat next to each other on the big rock. Their legs were hanging over the edge of the rock, and the tree branches above sheltered them from the scorching sun.

"Hey, I can see my house from here," Jess pointed to the right.

"I used to always wonder who lived in that house..." Miranda said.

Jess smiled for a few moments, "I'm glad we met."

"Me too," Miranda rested her head against Jess' shoulder.

The brunette loved that Miranda felt comfortable enough to put her head on her shoulder. She also enjoyed the fruity fragrance of Miranda's hair. It took her by surprise when Miranda put her hand in hers, a minute later. Jess' heart flooded with warmth as she held her friend's soft hand. She also found herself feeling very protective of her.

They sat like that for several minutes, and then the blue-haired woman raised her head.

"Have some tea with me?" Miranda asked.

"Okay," Jess whispered.

Once inside, they took towels from the closet, dried off and changed. Jess put on her T-shirt and shorts and Miranda wore a short, pink cotton dress. The two young women then went into the kitchen. After putting on the electric kettle, Miranda took out cups, plates and two green tea bags. She then took out a loaf of banana bread from the refrigerator and asked Jess to cut two slices for them.

They took their banana bread slices and tea to the porch and sat down at the little table. Both sat facing the direction of the lake. The breezes were a bit stronger and it helped to dry their damp hair. Jess took a bite of the banana bread.

"My mom made it," Miranda said before putting a piece into her mouth.

"It's excellent," Jess commented.

"I like cooking a lot, but some dishes and desserts I just don't trust myself with…"

The brunette chuckled, "We should cook together sometime."

"That would be wonderful," Miranda responded. "Maybe we can prepare lunch tomorrow?"

"Tomorrow is good," Jess said. "Should I bring anything?"

"No, you don't have to bring anything," the blue-haired woman said. "I have some raw fish fillets… I'm thinking we could do something with them. Also have some potatoes, canned vegetables, salt, vegetable oil and some seasonings."

Jess nodded and thought of the possibilities, given those ingredients. A long silence followed as Miranda remembered the beautiful cat that met her on the porch a few days ago.

"You know, that day we met," Miranda said, "I wasn't really hiking. The cat, Oliver, he wanted me to follow him so I did… He led me to your home."

"Oh," Jess raised her eyebrows. "Sweet Ollie was very strange… but in a good way."

"How was Ollie strange?"

"It felt like he could understand everything we were saying, and knew all that was happening."

Miranda started sipping her tea, "I don't doubt you."

When the young women were finished having tea, they collected the dishes and cups and went inside. After they helped each other wash the used dishes and cups, Jess said that she needed to leave shortly, because she had to prepare dinner at home. The brunette could tell that Miranda was sad that she had to leave.

"I'll be here tomorrow at 11 am," Jess assured her, at the front door. "I really like spending time with you, Miranda."

There was vulnerability in Jess's voice that lit a fire within Miranda's chest.

"I like spending time with you too, Jess."

Suddenly, their eyes locked in an intense, magnetic gaze. Slowly, Jess stepped forward and kissed Miranda's lips, delicately. When the blue-haired woman felt Jess' soft and pretty mouth on hers, she closed her eyes and began to kiss her back. As they kissed, Jess gently cupped Miranda's cheek, and Miranda held her lightly at the waist. A few moments later, the brunette broke the kiss. Miranda opened her eyes and felt her head spinning in euphoria.

"I should go home and prepare dinner," Jess whispered.

Miranda nodded and looked on as her friend walked off the porch. They waved to each other before Jess turned the corner and disappeared.

Chapter 7

Jess showed up the following day a few minutes before 11am, dressed in a different pair of shorts and another T-shirt. She brought with her a knapsack with some items. When Miranda came out, they hugged warmly. Miranda had on denim shorts and a light yellow top. After they hugged, they went into the kitchen.

On a chair in the kitchen, the brunette rested her knapsack. She opened it and carefully pulled out a beautiful red rose. Smiling, she handed it to Miranda. Miranda's face flushed almost as red as the rose. After thanking her friend, she quickly filled a transparent glass with water and placed the stem of the flower in it. While she rested it in the living room, Jess took out a paper bag filled with about a dozen nectarines. When Miranda returned to the kitchen, she handed it to her.

"These are for you," Jess said. "They're from my tree."

"Thank you so much, Jess."

'If you want, I could use a few to make you a pie," Jess suggested. "I brought flour, sugar, cinnamon and a few other things just in case."

"A pie sounds like a wonderful idea," Miranda remarked.

After a minute of deciding what to prepare with the fish and potatoes, they spent about an hour, happily cooking together. The blue-haired woman observed Jess' passion in the kitchen and noticed she was quite talented.

The stove was small, but they managed very well. Jess seasoned and stewed the fish and Miranda oven-roasted the potatoes. It took about fifteen minutes for Jess to prepare the pie to bake. She put it in the oven while the potatoes were roasting and both the potatoes and the pie were finished at the same time. The cottage smelled amazing.

The meal was absolutely delicious. The stewed fish and potatoes were flavored perfectly, and the pie was the best fruit pie Miranda had ever tasted. It was just sweet enough, so the taste of the nectarines could be appreciated, and the amount of cinnamon was just right.

When they were done eating, they sat and talked for a bit.

"I can see you're very passionate about cooking," Miranda said. "And you're so good at it. I think you'd do really well if you open a restaurant."

"Thanks," Jess responded. "It's actually a goal of mine. Are you passionate about hairdressing?"

"I am," the blue-haired woman replied, "ever since I was little. I'm working towards owning my own salon."

"Do you do your own hair?" Jess asked.

"Yes, I dye my own hair."

"I love the colour."

"I brought some of the same dye with me, actually," Miranda said. "If you want I can do yours for you."

"Thanks, but I don't think it would suit me."

"How about I do just a strand, then?"

After seeing the excited look in Miranda's face, Jess agreed for her to dye a strand of her hair blue. Miranda seated her friend in the living room and then got what was necessary from her suitcase. In less than an hour, Miranda had finished. Jess checked out her hair in the bathroom mirror while Miranda stood behind her. The blue-haired woman asked what she thought of it. Jess replied that it looked cool. Miranda smiled and said she should go wash the dishes in the kitchen, and the brunette offered to help her.

There was a good amount of cleaning up to do in the kitchen. As Miranda wiped the table, Jess put what needed to be washed into the sink. Jess washed the dishes while her friend rinsed them and packed them in their places.

They were surprised at how fast they completed the task. When Miranda turned to get a small kitchen towel for them to dry their hands, she felt Jess' strong arms gently wrap around her waist from behind. As the blue-haired woman melted in Jess' embrace, Jess kissed her ear, and then her cheek, softly. Miranda's began to feel her heart pounding in her chest. She turned around and pressed her lips against Jess'. When the brunette felt Miranda's lips part, she slipped her tongue into her mouth. Their bodies were on fire as their tongues wrestled together.

Taking Jess' hand, Miranda pulled her to the couch. There, she had Jess lie down and then she lay on top of her. The couch was very comfortable and roomy. As they started kissing again, they began grinding their bodies together. Reaching down, the blue-haired woman found the waistbands of Jess' shorts and panties and began pulling them downwards. Jess raised her buttocks off the sofa and helped her take them off. While Jess undid the button of Miranda's denim shorts, Miranda admired Jess' beautiful and neatly trimmed pussy. She could see that Jess was very moist. Jess then helped the blue-haired woman pull her denim shorts and white lace panties off her legs. Miranda's hairless and smooth pussy glistened with her wetness.

As the young women gazed into each other's eyes, their legs entwined and they pressed their pussies together. When their clits touched for the first time, a jolt of intense pleasure shot through both of their bodies. Miranda began to rock her hips, causing their slippery pussy lips and swollen clits to rub together. Jess held her by the waist and moved her body too. Soon they established a rhythm. Jess bit her lip as she felt her orgasm approaching. Miranda was close too. When the blue-haired woman began to come, she threw her head back and started moaning. As her orgasm intensified, she moaned even louder and this triggered Jess' orgasm. Jess grabbed her lover's buttocks with her strong hands as they both trembled in ecstasy. Warm, delicious waves of pleasure coursed through their bodies for nearly a minute.

When they came down from heaven, they kissed breathlessly, and then the blue-haired woman lay on top of Jess, with her head on the brunette's chest. Jess kissed the top of Miranda's head and slowly stroked her hair. They lay like that, with their legs still entwined, and feeling the other's heartbeats for many minutes.

"I've never come like that," Miranda murmured. "That was... mind-blowing."

"It was, for me, too."

"Would you like to go for a swim?" Miranda said, sitting up.

"Sure," Jess smiled. "I packed a bath suit just in case you asked me."

Miranda changed into her two-piece bath suit while Jess fetched hers from the car. Jess returned with a navy-blue two-piece. The tag at the back of the top half showed she had never worn it. After Jess changed into the two-piece, Miranda thought the brunette looked very sexy in it.

For an hour, they had a lot of fun in the clear, cool lake. They kissed often and found it hard to keep their hands off of each other. Miranda had never felt so alive in her life. The late afternoon found them sitting on the big rock, with Miranda's head on Jess' shoulder.

"I have something to tell you," Jess whispered. "It's something about me..."

Miranda took Jess' hand, "Is what you have to tell me good, or bad?"

"Neither, it's just something I think you should know," Jess replied. "It's also something no one else knows."

"What is it?" Miranda raised her head and looked at Jess.

"I have a penis."

"You mean you have a dildo."

"No, I have a real penis," Jess looked down between her own legs and then looked into her lover's blue eyes.

Miranda could tell Jess was serious.

"Are you talking about your clit?" Miranda asked.

Jess shook her head, "It's inside me, and I'm able to push it out from a slit that's right above the opening of my vagina."

Miranda couldn't believe what she was hearing, however she found the idea of it very sexually arousing.

"Can I... see it?"

"I'll show it to you for a little while," Jess said.

After the brunette scanned the area to ensure that there were no signs of anyone nearby, she slowly pulled the bottom of her navy-blue two-piece down to her knees. Keeping her eyes fixed between Jess' legs, Miranda felt her heart start to beat faster. Placing her hands behind herself on the rock for support, Jess spread her legs a little and leaned back a bit. Miranda's eyes widened as a thick, pink and erect phallus emerged from right beneath Jess' clit. Its head was large and it extended about a foot from Jess vagina. It was covered in veins and natural lubrication. The blue-haired woman was speechless.

"You're the only person I've told about this," Jess said. "Not even my mother knows."

Miranda watched as Jess withdrew her phallus back into its slit and pulled up the bottom of her bath suit.

"Did you always know about it?" Miranda finally found her voice.

"I realized I had it when I was 11," the brunette replied. "I dreamed I was having sex with some girl and when I woke up, I saw something pitched a tent between my legs. When I removed the covers and looked down, I was so shocked to see I had a huge penis. I felt like I needed to rub it, badly, so I went to the washroom and started to rub it. I came after a few minutes... A lot of clear liquid spurted out."

"Do you know if you can get a woman pregnant?"

"I wondered the same thing," Jess said. "Then, when I was 15, I ejaculated everyday for a few months and checked the liquid under a microscope my mother has in the storage room at home. I only saw sperm once for the month. It didn't take me long to figure out that my body produced sperm only during a new moon."

"Interesting..."

"Anyway, I searched through books for answers to why I was like this, and just last year, I found the information I was looking for."

"What did you find?" Miranda inquired. "And how did you get the information?"

"There's an old, wooden chest in the storage room," said the brunette." My mother keeps it locked and she always has the key with her. I found a way to break into it and fix it back so no one would notice that it was broken into... In that chest I found her old diary. It's one she had years before I was born. My mother never mentioned much about my father, but in that diary I found out about him."

"What about him?"

"He wasn't from here," Jess replied. "He was from another planet. My mother used a ritual to summon him when she was in her twenties. According to what she wrote in those pages, he had black hair and blue eyes. He was good-looking, but he wasn't... *good*. He used to appear at night in her room and they used to sleep together. After he got my mother pregnant, he left her about three months later. One month after that, I was born. I weighed five pounds and was healthy."

"Maybe the reason why your mother's magic is so powerful is because he helps her," the blue-haired woman said.

"I was thinking that," Jess responded. "Maybe you're right... Anyway, I have to find a way to stop my mother from harming anyone else."

"Have you tried searching for ways on the internet?"

"Yes, but there isn't much information about what I'm looking for on the internet," said the brunette. "Tomorrow afternoon, I'd like to check out some more books at the library, especially in the room we were in. Would you come with me?"

"Yes, I'll go with you," Miranda smiled.

Jess returned the smile and then informed her lover that she had to leave to help her grandfather with something. They then got up, went into the cottage and changed into dry clothes. At the door, before the brunette left, they exchanged cell-phone numbers and then kissed each other's lips. Leaning against an open widow inside of the cottage, Miranda watched as Jess got into her white pickup and drove off.

Chapter 8

The next day, a few minutes after 2 in the afternoon, Jess picked up Miranda near at her cottage. The blue-haired woman gave Jess a hug before buckling up. As soon as the brunette started driving, she remembered that she had forgotten her phone at home. She decided to drive up to her home and retrieve it.

When Jess reached her home, she parked at the side of the road in front of the yellow house. She then told Miranda she was going to get her phone and would return quickly. Seconds after the brunette went inside, Miranda felt as if she was being watched. Looking up, the blue-haired woman saw Jess' mother angrily peering down at her from the banister. The middle-aged woman was much scarier than Miranda had pictured in her mind. She was a lanky woman with a hard face, and her lips were tightly pressed together in a forbidding expression. Above her long, hooked nose were evil, piercing eyes and thick brows which met in the middle. It seemed the only thing she had in common with Jess was that they had the same colour brown hair.

A few moments later, the front door opened and Jess exited holding her phone. Miranda breathed a sigh of relief when she saw the brunette. She looked up and saw that Jess' mother was no longer there.

Jess restarted the engine and looked over at Miranda. She could tell that Miranda was tense.

"You Okay?" Jess gently squeezed Miranda's arm.

"Yeah…"

The brunette took her girlfriend's hand and used the other to drive.

On the way to the library, Jess spotted someone inside of a small café and stopped right next to it.

"Someone would like to meet you," Jess smiled.

Miranda knew who the brunette was referring to. As soon as they entered the café, the blue-haired woman immediately recognized the old man who was at a table on the left. He recognized her also. It was Jess' grandfather. They were all joyful to see one another. They all beamed and then the two ladies joined him at the table.

Jess' grandfather looked very fresh and cheerful. His hair was tied in a ponytail and he wore a lime-green shirt with khaki trousers. He was having a late lunch. In front of him was a large sandwich and at the side of him was a cup of hot green tea. He offered to buy the young women lunch, but they told him they had already eaten. He then ordered two fruit punches for Miranda and Jess.

"You'd love the fruit punch," Jess looked at Miranda. "They make their own and it's delicious."

"I'm happy you ladies came to see me," he said as the waitress placed the drinks on the table. "I want to thank you both... I don't have words to tell you how grateful I am."

"I'm glad everything is Okay now with you," Miranda said. "You look so happy and healthy now and it's really wonderful to see that."

Jess's grandfather smiled briefly, and then his expression turned solemn.

"I wish my daughter would leave the path she's on," he said. "Jessie told me she's been trying to find a spell or ritual to prevent her from harming more people... To stop what she's doing, Annie needs to want to stop. She has to want to change her ways," he shook his head, "and I don't think there's a spell that can do that..."

"There must be a way," Jess was determined.

Jess' grandfather nodded after drinking some of his tea.

"I trust that you ladies will be careful."

"We will," Miranda replied.

"Although my daughter won't do anything to intentionally harm me, I know I must be careful too."

At 3 pm, they arrived at the library. In the room at the library, they began to thoroughly search the shelves for books that would help them in rendering a black magician powerless. In less than half of an hour, they found over two dozen books that they thought would be helpful, and stacked them on the table. After taking half of the books, Miranda sat down next to Jess. They hardly talked as they looked through the pages of those old books. Two hours later, Jess informed Miranda that she had found something in a book and moved it closer to Miranda so that they both can read what the brunette had found.

"It's a ritual…" The blue-haired woman observed. "Does it involve summoning any entities?"

"No," Jess replied. "It's to prevent someone's magic from working… I'd have to write this spell down nine times on white paper, and include my mother's full name. Then, I need to draw this symbol over it, in red, place it in the light of a full moon for at least an hour, and then burn the paper."

"The moon will be full tonight…"

"Yes, I'll do this tonight."

Jess pulled out her notebook and started writing down some information from the opened book in front of her. Afterwards, they checked the few remaining books they had collected. The only useful piece of information they found was that one ritual. When it was nearly 6 pm, they left the library.

On the way back, Miranda invited Jess to have dinner with her at the cottage and she agreed. Shortly afterwards, Jess received a call from her grandfather. After the brief conversation, Miranda asked who it was.

"That was my granddad," the brunette closed her flip phone. "He said he was picking up dinner and wanted to know what I'd like. I told him I'd be having dinner at your place."

When they got to the cottage, Jess rested her bag down on the sofa and Miranda changed into a cream, short cotton dress. Jess offered to cook diner. After checking out the ingredients that were in the kitchen, Jess realized that Miranda had bought a variety of nice vegetables from the farmer's market. She decided to make Pasta Primavera.

Dinner was fantastic. The blue-haired woman had the dish before, but the way Jess had flavoured it blew her mind. Miranda let Jess know how wonderful her cooking was and how much she appreciated it.

After they were finished washing up in the kitchen after dinner, they sat in the front porch, on the floor. It was a quiet and warm night. The full moon could be clearly seen through the branches of the huge tree in front of them. Miranda put her head on Jess' shoulder and they chatted for a bit.

A little while later, the brunette said it was time she returned home. At that moment, they got up, held each other and shared a kiss. It was meant to be a quick kiss on the lips, but it soon turned sensual and intense. Closing their eyes, they got swept away in the passion of that kiss.

The blue-haired woman felt a craving like she had never felt before. Feeling the strong heat in her lover's body, Jess put her hand under Miranda's short dress and began to rub her hot pussy through her soft panties. The brunette's fingers were pressing into Miranda's wet lips with just enough pressure, and moving at a pace that was driving Miranda wild.

"Jess... I want you... I *need* you inside me," Miranda's tone was soft but urgent.

Jess knew what her girlfriend meant, and wanted to satisfy her more than anything. Taking Jess by the hand, Miranda led her into the bedroom. The room was beautifully lit by the rays of the moon which came through the screened window. Soft breezes blew the parted curtains.

Standing in front of the bed, they started kissing and undressing each other. Taking the bottom of Miranda's dress, the brunette pulled it up and over her head, and let it fall to the floor. Then, the blue-haired woman helped Jess out of her grey T-shirt and then undid the belt on her pair of blue denim jeans. After Jess stepped out of her jeans, she was only in her bra and panties, like Miranda. Jess unhooked the back of her lover's bra and gently removed it. Pausing for a few moments, she admired her lover's beautiful C cup sized breasts, with their pink, erect nipples. She then peeled Miranda's wet panties off her pussy and down her legs.

Gracefully, Jess picked her lover up and rested her on the bed. Miranda was amazed at how strong the brunette was. Afterwards, she took off her own bra and panties and laid them on her jeans on the floor. Jess' breasts were a bit smaller and firmer than the blue-haired woman's.

As soon as Jess got into bed with Miranda, their hands began to eagerly explore each other's bodies. Lying side by side, they kissed hungrily and caressed each other's breasts and tummies. Miranda rolled on top of the brunette and took her left nipple into her mouth. While she sucked on Jess' stiff nipple, she massaged the other breast with her hand. After Miranda did this for about a minute, Jess turned her on her back and climbed on top of her.

Jess kissed her mouth passionately and then began to move down her body. She bit and sucked the soft skin of Miranda's neck before sucking and kneading both of her lover's breasts. Miranda felt herself getting even wetter. Heading lower, Jess licked and nibbled on all of the right places of Miranda's tummy, causing her to squirm, giggle and sigh. Soon, she arrived at the juncture of Miranda's thighs. She felt as if she could get addicted to the aroma of Miranda's very hot and moist pussy. In the moonlight, she was able to see Miranda's swollen clit, begging desperately for attention. The blue-haired woman shuddered when Jess' soft lips made contact with her clit. When Miranda's clit was engulfed in Jess' mouth, Jess felt it twitch. Miranda held the back of Jess' head and moaned as the brunette began to circle her clit with her tongue.

Moments later, while still pleasing Miranda's clit, Jess began to introduce her index finger into her lover's channel. Miranda was so tight. To Jess, it felt like Miranda had never had more than a finger inside of her pussy. Pressing upwards, she felt the blue-haired woman's engorged G-spot. Right afterwards, she found Miranda's little rosebud with her middle finger and rubbed it. Miranda made a surprised sound as Jess pressed her middle finger into her anus. The brunette fingered Miranda and sucked her clit until she was close, then she stopped and withdrew her fingers. She then kneeled between her legs and spread them. Miranda watched as about nine inches of Jess' large phallus emerged from its slit. It looked like a human penis, however, it was thicker and longer than the average human penis. It curved upwards and glistened with natural lubrication. She then mounted Miranda and rested her hands on the bed, at both sides of the blue-haired woman's head. Miranda ran her hands up and down Jess' washboard abs. She could feel the muscles under her rose petal-soft skin.

Using just her hips, Jess put the head of her cock against the entrance of Miranda's vagina. For a brief moment, Miranda was concerned about its size, but her desire to be penetrated by the brunette's penis was greater than her fear of pain. She took a deep breath and tried to relax fully. As Jess began to ease into Miranda, she felt the resistance of her lover's hymen. When she pushed in some more, Miranda felt a sharp pain and whimpered. Jess paused, and resting her weight on one hand, used the other to rub Miranda's arm to soothe her. While doing this, Jess tried to come up with a way that would be the least painful for Miranda, and then had a good idea. When she felt the blue-haired woman was calm, she kissed her left ear and sucked its lobe. Then, in an instant, she bit Miranda's lobe to distract her, and with one fast, but controlled thrust of her hips, pushed the head of her cock through the delicate membrane. Miranda gasped in pain, and as soon as she did, Jess covered her mouth with hers. The brunette reached down with one hand, and gently caressed the inside of Miranda's thigh. After giving Miranda some time to adjust, Jess moved her hips to gradually fill up her lover's pussy.

Miranda loved the feeling of Jess' thick and throbbing penis inside of her, and Jess enjoyed the way Miranda's tight, warm and slippery channel gripped her cock. The brunette began to rock her hips slowly at first. This caused amazing and delicious sensations inside of Miranda's vagina. They both moaned as Jess's cock massaged Miranda's sensitive walls and rubbed her enlarged G-spot with every thrust. They were so connected with each other that they were feeling each other's pleasure. When Jess increased the pace, the blue-haired woman held her at the waist.

Jess kissed her lover as she kept pumping into her. A few minutes later, Miranda felt a hot ball of ecstasy inside of her pussy and realized she was about to have her first vaginal orgasm. Miranda wrapped her arms around the brunette. Jess felt Miranda's need for her to go faster, so she did. Jess was very close to coming too. As they looked deeply into each other's eyes, the blue-haired woman noticed that Jess' hazel eyes were glowing in arousal. Seconds later, Miranda's fell into utter bliss and her pussy started to contract over and over again. While this was happening, her whole body tensed and then trembled. Jess began to come the same time Miranda did. Every cell of her body experienced intense pleasure as her cock spasmed and squirted copious amounts of her hot semen inside of her lover's vagina and womb. Miranda felt Jess' hot cum hitting her walls and entering her vagina. Their orgasms lasted for about a minute. Neither of them had ever come like that.

A short while afterwards, Jess slowly withdrew and then lit the lamp on the night stand. She got some tissues from a box right next to it, and began to wipe the warm semen that was leaking out of Miranda's vagina. Soon, Jess noticed a little blood on the tissues.

"What is it?" Miranda asked when she saw Jess studying the tissues.

"There's a bit of blood on the tissues," Jess whispered. "Are you in any pain?"

"I'm a little sore, but I'm Okay."

"Are you sure?"

"Yes."

After she finished wiping Miranda's vagina, Jess went to the washroom and flushed the napkins. She returned quickly and climbed up next to her lover. They kissed and lay in each other's arms for nearly an hour. At some time, the blue-haired woman drifted off to sleep. When it was about 9:30 pm, Jess pressed the light button on her watch. After seeing the time, she gently woke Miranda and told her she had to get home to perform the ritual. She told Miranda to remain in bed and then got dressed. After she put her clothes on, Jess gave her lover a kiss, and then made her way home.

Chapter 9

A few minutes after Jess left, Miranda locked up and went to sleep. When it was about 3 am, the blue-haired woman woke up to an eerie and heavy feeling. The room was unusually chilly. Suddenly, she saw something move at the foot of the bed. It was a blur at first and appeared to be a human being.

"Jess, is that you?" Miranda felt her heart thumping against her chest.

The being remained silent and then swiftly came over to Miranda's side of the bed. When she recognized what it was, she froze in terror. Angrily glaring down at her with its white glowing eyes was a dark hooded entity. In a second, it grabbed her by the neck. Frantically, Miranda tried hitting and kicking it, but her arms and legs just went straight through the entity. Its long black nails dug painfully into her neck as it tightened its grip. Gasping for air, she struggled desperately to escape the entity but it held her so tightly she couldn't move from where she was. She tried screaming but it was to no avail. As she felt herself lapsing into unconsciousness, she saw the room fading out.

Right as she was about to black out, she thought of something. With the last ounce of her strength, Miranda reached by the nightstand and hit the repellant Jess had made as hard as she could. When the glass vial landed on the floor, it broke. The liquid flowed out and its strong smell flooded the room. Immediately, the entity let go and drew back as if repulsed. Holding her own neck, Miranda started to cough and catch her breath. She watched as the entity quickly went through the bedroom wall and into another room. From the bedroom, Miranda heard loud sounds of breaking and smashing coming from other parts of the cottage, but she stayed put. After a couple of minutes, the noises ceased and the place was quiet again.

The blue-haired woman didn't go back to sleep. She stayed awake in bed and when it was dawn, she felt safe enough to leave the room. As soon as she entered the living room, she noticed a wooden shelf was completely ripped from the wall. The shelf, books, framed photos and the other items that were on the shelf lay on the floor. She saw a wooden chair was broken to pieces and a few plates were smashed. Miranda looked on the living room table at the rose Jess had given her. Its petals were brown and dry as if it had been there for several months. Next to the rose was her cell phone. She was relieved to find it in one piece. She picked it up and hurriedly sent a text message to Jess, asking her to come over as soon as possible.

Half an hour later, the brunette arrived at the cottage to find Miranda sitting in the porch, looking pale and upset. Jess went up to her and wrapped her in her arms. For the moments Jess held her, she felt completely safe.

"Thanks for coming," Miranda's voice broke.

"What happened?" Jess looked into Miranda's eyes.

Miranda described what had happened and revealed the marks and scratches on her neck. Jess became furious. The blue-haired woman then took Jess into the cottage and showed her the damage the entity had caused.

"This is my fault," Jess turned her anger to herself.

"It's not," Miranda shook her head.

"Yes, I shouldn't have done the ritual."

"I don't think it was the ritual, Jess," Miranda swallowed. "Your mom… she saw me when you went for your phone yesterday. She looked very angry."

"I shouldn't have parked so near to the house."

"Stop blaming yourself baby," Miranda touched Jess' face and looked into her smoldering eyes.

"No matter what happens, I will protect you," Jess looked at her lover reassuringly. "You're my girl and I won't let anything happen to you. Do you trust me?"

Miranda nodded and then they embraced for a while. Afterwards, Miranda made coffee for both of them. Sitting in the living room with their hot beverages, they tried to think of a way to solve the problem.

"Maybe I should just leave," Miranda said.

"It would find you," Jess said. "It would keep visiting you at night, wherever you are until it does what it was sent to do."

"At night..."

"Yes, they come out only during the night," the brunette informed her.

"Because the daylight would destroy them..."

"We'd need to find a way to get it in the sunlight," Jess pondered.

"Maybe we should check the library again?" Miranda suggested.

"We've been through every book there that had to do with evil spirits," Jess responded.

About three-quarters of an hour later, frustration began to set in for both of them. They knew they had to come up with something before nightfall.

Jess looked at Miranda, "There is someone who I think might be able to help us..." Jess' voice lacked confidence.

"Who is this person?" Miranda asked.

"She's a forty-something-year-old witch who lives about ten minutes' drive from here."

"Why haven't you mentioned this before?"

"My mother said she's evil and warned me never to go near the place."

"Do you believe your mother?"

"I don't trust my mother, but I'm still wary of the woman," Jess replied. "Her name is Eugenia. She sells vegetables at the market every Sunday. She looks a bit eccentric and her energy… is intense."

"We should pay her a visit," Miranda was hopeful.

Jess sighed, "It seems like the only option we have."

Chapter 10

After having a quick breakfast of eggs and toast, they got into Jess' pickup and began to make their way to Eugenia's home. It was a cool morning. The sky was completely overcast and there was a strange tension in the air. A few minutes later, Jess turned into a dirt road and had to pause for a farmer and about two dozen sheep to cross. The woods were thicker in that area and there were no houses along that stretch. Lightning flashed across the sky, and a loud rumbling of thunder followed. Suddenly, the brunette took a sharp left turn onto a steep road. When Miranda looked up, she saw an old wooden farmhouse some distance away.

"We're almost there," Jess drove slowly.

Jess parked in front of the house, right next to a grey van, and then they both got out. The house was surrounded by clumps of trees and at the side of it, there was a kitchen garden. Behind the place were farm animals and a huge cleared area on which different crops were planted. An old and ornery cream coloured mixed-breed dog was relaxing on the patio near the front door. As the couple walked up the three stairs to the patio, she raised her head. The brunette straightened her shirt and politely knocked three times on the door. Moments later, a robust middle-aged man with black shiny hair answered the door. He wore a vest and brown trousers and looked at them as if he wasn't used to visitors.

"Good morning," Jess said. "We came to see Eugenia… Is she at home?"

He turned to look inside, "Gene, there are two girls here to see you!"

A few moments later, Eugenia came to the door. She was a slim woman with dark brown hair and very focused Emerald green eyes. She wore a loose fitting purple dress, necklaces of crystals and beads and a serious but pleasant expression.

"Hi, my name is Jess and this is my friend Miranda," Jess began. "We're in some trouble and think you might be able to help us."

"What kind of trouble are you in?"

"There's an evil spirit that nearly took my friend's life," Jess replied. "We don't know how to rid of it."

"Come in," Eugenia said.

Eugenia led them up the creaky stairs and into her study. After inviting them to have a seat next to each other at her desk, she lit a stick of sage incense and sat on the other side of the desk. There were several shelves of books behind them, some old watercolour paintings on the walls and a gorgeous palm-sized Celestitie geode in front of them on the desk. A thick light-yellow curtain was tied up midway with a white ribbon in front of an opened window.

"I will do what I can to help you girls," the middle-aged woman said. "Tell me what happened."

Miranda told Eugenia about what had happened and showed her the marks on her neck. Eugenia's eyes expressed concern.

"It's certain that someone sent this spirit to kill you," Eugenia said to Miranda. "Do you suspect anyone?"

"We suspect it's my mother," Jess replied with a hint of anger in her voice.

"Annie…" Eugenia whispered.

"You know my mother?"

"We were best friends."

"You were?" Jess was surprised. "How come she never told me this?"

"She hates me," Eugenia remarked.

"What happened between you?" Jess was curious.

After pouring them all some green tea, Eugenia began to enlighten them about her and Annie's shared history.

"We grew up together," she started. "We even went to the same high school. After high school, she went to college and I decided to get married and do farming which is one of my passions. She wanted to become a scientist. Right after college, she told me her dream changed and she wanted most of all to become a witch. I was interested in witchcraft too. We were interested in the same thing, but our intentions were different." She sat back in her chair and continued, "We sought advice from my grandmother who was a white witch. She told us what books and items we'd need to get and the good principles we'd need to abide by. She was very intuitive and had a gift to read people and tell their future. One day, and I remember it as if it was yesterday, she pulled me aside and told me that Annie would use witchcraft for evil purposes… Do you know who your father is, Jess?"

"She never told me, but I read about it in her diary."

"So you know he's not from this world."

"Yes."

"When we were in our twenties, she used to complain that her magic wasn't working," Eugenia took a sip of her tea. "Then, one night she called me and said she had summoned a male entity from another planet. I asked her if he was good and she joked that he was good only in bed. I realized she had crossed over onto the evil path, just as my grandmother had told me… She said he had given her a ring that would help her get things she wanted."

"Is it the black Obsidian ring she wears all the time?"

"It's not Obsidian, dear," Eugenia replied. "It's a mineral that's foreign to the Earth… Anyway, he left her a few months after he impregnated her, and she hates me because she thinks I have something to do with it."

"Did you?" Jess asked.

"No," she said. "I warned her many times about him but didn't do anything to make him leave."

"Both of my parents are evil," Jess looked down. "Maybe there's something wrong with me too…"

"I feel energies the way my grandmother did," Eugenia said, "and I know you're quite the opposite, dear. You have an extremely high vibration, similar to an angel's. Also, you chose to reincarnate here on Earth for a great purpose."

Jess felt the weight she had carried for years lift off of her. She was relieved, and also excited for the future.

"Do you know what I'm supposed to do?"

"No," Eugenia replied, "but in a few years, your gifts will unfold completely, and you will remember what you came here to do. Your friend Miranda is also like you and both of you will work together. I'm very happy you met each other."

Eugenia looked at both of them and gave a knowing smile. Jess and Miranda both blushed when they realized she knew they were together.

"That ring your mother wears, that's the source of her power," Eugenia said. "The spirits she sends to do her bidding and harm others stay inside that ring during the day. They are very powerful spirits... Do you think you can remove the ring from her while she's asleep?"

"I'll try," Jess said, "but my mother is a light sleeper."

Eugenia got up and opened a small cabinet behind her. She took out a small packet of dried herbs.

"Boil this in water and add about a tablespoon of the liquid to her food or drink this evening before dark," she handed the packet to the brunette. "It will make her fall asleep in ten minutes and keep her asleep for approximately fourteen hours. This will give you enough time to do the following ritual and place the ring back on her finger before she wakes up."

The young women listened carefully as Eugenia gave them the instructions for the ritual.

"You'd need to remove her ring while she's asleep and immediately put it into a clear glass bottle of the repellent you make, and seal the bottle. But before placing it in the liquid in the bottle, draw this symbol on the front and cork of the bottle," Eugenia quickly drew a symbol on paper and slid it over to Jess. "This symbol will keep the spirits imprisoned in the bottle after they have been driven out of the ring by the repellant. Make sure you place the ring in the bottle of repellant before the sun sets, and make sure to seal the bottle right after dropping the ring inside.

Afterwards, put the bottle outside and wait for the sun's rays at dawn to fall upon it. Let it sit in the morning sun for a few minutes, then open the bottle, take the ring out of it, discard the bottle and its contents, rinse the ring out with water and put the ring back on Annie's finger."

Miranda and Jess were very grateful for Eugenia's help. They offered to pay Eugenia but she refused the money and said they were welcome to visit her anytime. Before leaving, the brunette informed Eugenia that she'd let her know how the ritual went.

Chapter 11

On their way back, the rain started to pour down. Jess parked a short distance away from her house. She told Miranda she'd be back in a few minutes. Jess returned five minutes later and handed her a vial of repellant.

"Keep this with you in case of anything," Jess said. "After I drop you at the cottage, I have to go home to prepare lunch and in the afternoon, I have a job to do with my granddad. When I'm finished, I'll make dinner at home and give my mother the sedative in her tea. I'll draw the symbol on the two places on the bottle and as soon as she falls asleep, I'll remove the ring, put it in the bottle of repellant and bring it to the cottage before dark."

Miranda nodded and then Jess restarted the engine. When they got to the cottage, Jess held Miranda's hand, kissed it gently and reassured her that she would return that evening before the sun went down.

The blue-haired woman had lunch and then spent a good chunk of the afternoon reading and watching the rain fall on the lake from the porch. Before she knew it, the sun had started to set. After realizing that it was getting dark, she checked the time on her phone and called her girlfriend. The phone rang a few times and then went to voicemail. Miranda began to panic. She opened the vial that Jess had given her and sprinkled some repellant in every room. When it was dusk, Miranda tried phoning the brunette again, but got no answer. Less than a minute later, she heard Jess call from the porch. She quickly opened the door and invited her in.

After resting her bag on the couch, the brunette unzipped it and pulled out a clear glass bottle filled with the light-green repellant. The bottle was about the size of a beer bottle and had a wooden cork at the top. Carefully, she handed it to Miranda. The blue-haired woman noticed a symbol written on the front and cork of the bottle. At the bottom of the bottle, she saw a large ring.

"She fell asleep on the sofa a minute after she drank the tea," Jess said. "I told my grandfather what we were doing, so he won't try to wake her."

"I tried calling you," Miranda said, "but you didn't answer…"

"Oh, I didn't know you tried to call," the brunette replied. "I put my phone on silent so it won't wake her."

Miranda looked outside, "There's a place on the huge rock by the lake that gets direct sunlight at sunrise."

Jess accompanied her to the rock and they rested the bottle in a small indentation on the rock where the sun would hit it. They shook it lightly to make sure it was secure and went inside.

"You'll stay the night, I hope," the blue-haired woman looked at Jess.

"I will."

"Do you think it would work?" Miranda asked.

"I hope so," Jess began taking a few tools out of her bag. "Time would tell."

"What are those tools for?"

"I'm going to repair your shelf and chair."

"Thank you so much," Miranda said. "Can I help?"

"Sure."

After they were finished repairing the furniture, Miranda made dinner for both of them while Jess took a shower. They went to bed early so they could wake up at dawn.

"I'll be leaving tomorrow evening," Miranda whispered as she lay close to Jess.

"I'm leaving here soon, too." Jess put her arm around her lover. "But for good. I already told my grandfather. I can't stay another day at that house... with that woman."

"Where would you go?"

"Somewhere in the city," Jess replied. "I have enough money to rent an apartment while I look for a job.

"Come stay with me at my apartment," Miranda said. "You'd like it there."

"I'd like anywhere as long as I'm with you," Jess replied. "But I don't want to be a burden."

"It would be a burden if you're not with me," Miranda held her lover's hand.

"I feel the same way," Jess said. "...I'll stay with you."

They kissed and then drifted off to sleep. Right before dawn, Miranda felt a weight on her chest. When she opened her eyes, she was surprised to see Oliver sitting on her and staring into her eyes.

"Jess!"

"Mmm..." Jess opened her eyes and was astonished and elated to see Oliver sitting on top of Miranda.

Oliver purred and allowed them to pet him for a few moments, and then he lovingly meowed and jumped down. When they got up and looked around the room, they realized he disappeared.

"I think he wanted to wake us up," Jess smiled. "He used to do this on mornings when I had school."

"Look, the sun is rising," the blue-haired woman said as she watched out the window. "Let's check the bottle."

Miranda and Jess stood next to each other by the rock and watched as the rising sun started to bathe the bottle with its bright rays. They planned to let it sit there for a few minutes in the dawn's direct sunlight, as Eugenia had instructed them to do. After a minute in the sun, the bottle started to shake.

"Are you seeing that?" Miranda was shocked.

Jess was speechless. They moved closer to the rock and looked on. For half of a minute, the bottle vibrated as if it was filled with a hundred angry bugs from hell. Then, it suddenly stood still, and within a few moments, all of the light-green repellant became black. Three minutes later, Jess walked up to the rock and picked up the bottle. When she pulled out the cork, the liquid inside gave off a bad odour. It smelled like ashes and rotten eggs. A moment later, dozens of little lights of different colours flew out of the bottle like fireflies. The lights flew upwards and then disappeared in seconds.

"What was that?" Miranda asked.

"I don't know," responded Jess, "but maybe Eugenia would be able to tell us. We should visit her today and let her know what happened."

Jess quickly went inside and flushed the foul liquid down the toilet. She then removed the ring and discarded the bottle. Right after washing the ring out with water, Jess went home and found her mother snoring on the living room couch. She slipped the ring back on her finger and returned to the cottage.

The morning was fresh, light and beautiful. After eating breakfast, they made their way to Eugenia's place. As they sat in her study, they told Eugenia how the ritual went. The middle-aged woman was glad to inform them that the ritual was successful. She said all of the evil spirits in the ring were destroyed.

"The lights that flew out of the bottle," Miranda said, "what were they?"

"Inside of the ring, Annie's evil spirits had imprisoned the souls of all of the people they had killed for her, and the ritual you girls performed freed them," Eugenia smiled.

"Why would the evil spirits keep the souls trapped there in the ring?

"They trapped them there so they could feed off of their energy," Eugenia replied.

That evening, Jess told her grandfather that she was leaving and would be staying with Miranda in the city. She told him he was welcome to visit anytime. After quickly packing her things into her pickup, the brunette drove to the cottage. There, she found Miranda already packed and ready to leave. As she followed Miranda's car with her pickup, she promised herself to never return to the yellow house.

That night, after Jess' mother found out that the brunette had left, she screamed and threw a massive tantrum. Jess' granddad found his daughter's behaviour was very funny but he didn't show her that he was laughing. That same night, she tried calling on her spirits but didn't get any response. She realized they were gone and knew Jess and her friend had something to do with it. That made her even angrier. Word soon got around that she had lost her powers and her business quickly dried up.

A few days after the couple had settled down in the apartment, Miranda took Jess to meet her parents and introduced her to them as her girlfriend. They immediately loved her. A week later, her father, a lecturer at a college there in the city helped her to get enrolled in the school's culinary arts program. Two years later, Miranda opened her own salon and a year after that, Jess started her own restaurant. Later that year, they got married, and all of their close friends and family including Jess' grandfather and Eugenia came to the beautiful ceremony.

If you loved this story or it moved you in any way, please don't hesitate to leave a review or feedback. Your thoughts will be helpful and appreciated very much.

My site where I post about myself, my books and new releases: https://authorliliahraye.wordpress.com

You can also find me, Liliah Raye, on Twitter.

To be added to my mailing list, send your email address to: sarahconnects85@yahoo.com

If you enjoyed this story, you might also like:

Nika
In this erotic romance novella, a portal takes Sarah, a young and beautiful high school teacher, to a heavenly planet called Aniki where she encounters its gorgeous hermaphrodite queen, Nika.
https://www.amazon.com/Nika-Liliah-Raye-ebook/dp/B07QDJ98H3

Stranger in the Woods
In this erotic futa and lesbian romance, Lily, a pretty and sweet 18-year-old redhead from a small town, meets a beautiful and mysterious woman in the woods outside her home.
https://www.amazon.com/dp/B07SY98J92

Oceana the Futa Mermaid (Alpha Futas of the Sea, Book 1)
In this erotic lesbian and futa romance, Valerie, a stunning, superficial and arrogant 20-year-old gets more than she expected after making a deal with a gorgeous and powerful mermaid.
https://www.amazon.com/dp/B084HHT5DN

Valerie the Futa Mermaid (Alpha Futas of the Sea, Book 2)
A serum gives Valerie bouts of extreme sexual desire for a few days. Her first mission with Oceana involves rescuing a rich and spoiled 18-year-old and escorting her home safely. Because of the serum, the blonde finds herself being insanely tempted by the young woman they're helping. Would she be able to resist temptation and stay faithful to her wife?
https://www.amazon.com/dp/B08DCC731P

I also wrote a book in which I revealed the steps I took to quickly and easily attract my twin flame. If you're on a quest to find your twin flame, the formula in the following book will work for you too:

How to Attract Your Twin Flame Quickly and Easily

The 7-step formula revealed in this book is what I used to call in my twin flame. When I completed the 7 steps of this formula, she came into my life like lightning.

Have you ever heard of the term twin flames? Twin flames are 2 souls who were originally 1 soul. At some point, that 1 soul was split into 2. When twin flames unite, they connect so deeply that they feel like 1 person.

In a twin flame relationship, there is a lot of love, respect, consideration, depth and spiritual growth happening. Twin flames are so happy together that they help other people be happy too. In fact, when twin flames unite on Earth, they raise the vibration of the whole planet. These are the reasons why so many persons want to find their twin flames.

It's Okay if you don't believe in twin flames. If you want to attract a romantic partner who'll help you have the greatest happiness and peace, this book will help you call them in, easily and quickly.

https://www.amazon.com/dp/B08B7ZHG1Z

Manufactured by Amazon.ca
Acheson, AB